Mama's Way

BY HELEN KETTEMAN

PICTURES BY MARY WHYTE

Dial Books for Young Readers NEW YORK

Published by Dial Books for Young Readers
A division of Penguin Putnam Inc.
345 Hudson Street
New York, New York 10014
Designed by Atha Tehon
Text set in Adobe Raleigh
Printed in Hong Kong on acid-free paper
1 3 5 7 9 10 8 6 4 2

Library of Congress Cataloging-in-Publication Data
Ketteman, Helen.
Mama's way/by Helen Ketteman; pictures by Mary Whyte.
p.   cm.
Summary: Wynona longs for a beautiful new dress to wear
to her sixth-grade graduation, even though she knows
her mama cannot afford to buy one for her.
ISBN 0-8037-2413-6
[1. Clothing and dress—Fiction. 2. Mothers and daughters—Fiction.]
I. Whyte, Mary, ill. II. Title.
PZ7.K484 Mam 2001   [E]—dc21   00-022929

The full color artwork was prepared
using watercolor washes.

For mothers and daughters
M.W. & H.K.

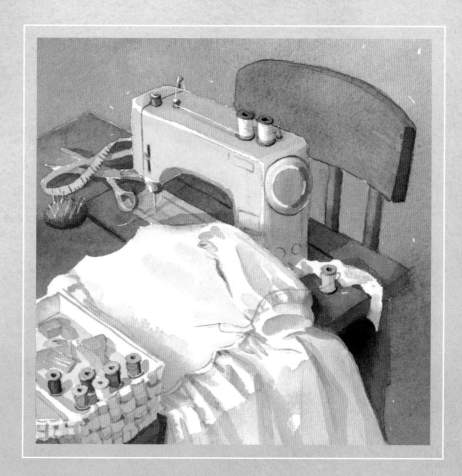

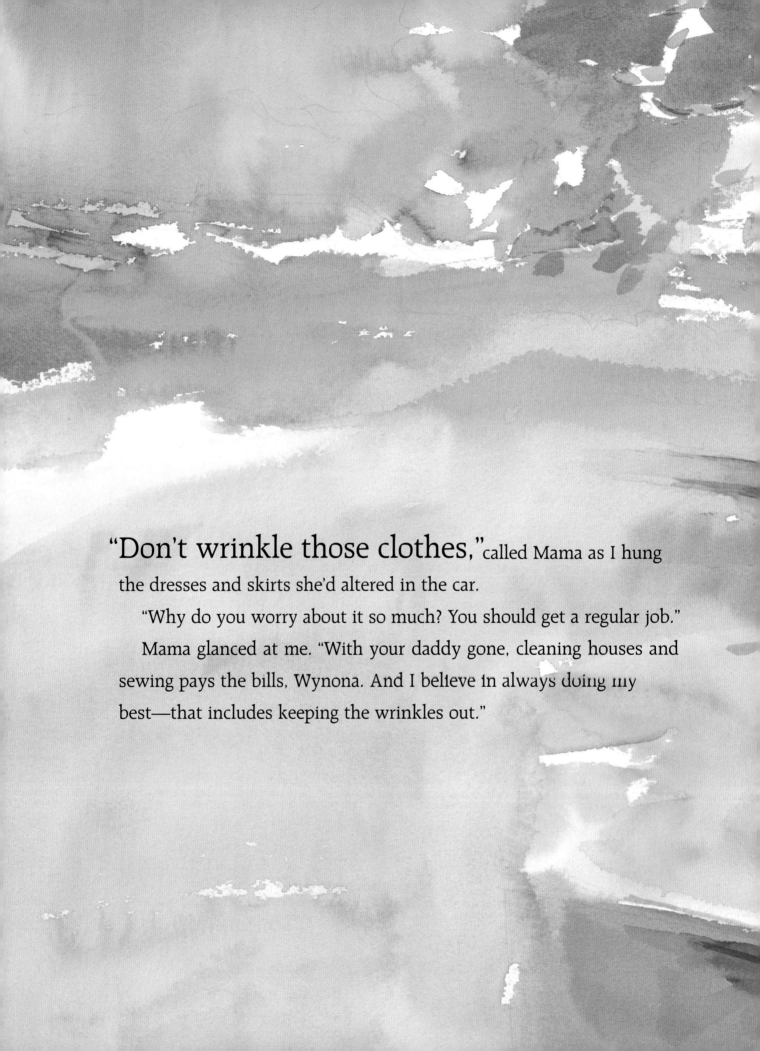

"Don't wrinkle those clothes," called Mama as I hung the dresses and skirts she'd altered in the car.

"Why do you worry about it so much? You should get a regular job."

Mama glanced at me. "With your daddy gone, cleaning houses and sewing pays the bills, Wynona. And I believe in always doing my best—that includes keeping the wrinkles out."

My younger brothers, Aaron and John Franklin, stayed with neighbors while Mama and I left to deliver the clothes to the Applebys.

Sarah, my friend from school, opened the door. She called her mother, then grabbed my hand. "I have a surprise for you, Wynona! Come upstairs!"

When we got to her room, she pulled a white dress from the closet. "Since sixth-grade graduation is coming up, I saved you this dress I outgrew. I wish I were as tiny as you."

I took it, blushing a little. I didn't have a white dress, and all the girls wore white at graduation. "It's pretty. Thanks," I said.

Then Sarah pulled out another dress. "This is my new graduation dress."

I gasped. It was the most beautiful dress I'd ever seen! Its silky white fabric swished when Sarah moved it. Delicate lace trimmed the collar and sleeves, and the sash was a pale blue velvet ribbon.

"Feel the velvet," said Sarah.

I shook my head. "M-my hands are dirty," I mumbled, balling up my fists.

The door opened, and Mama and Sarah's mother entered.

"Get the dress on, Sarah. Mrs. Anderson doesn't have all day."

While Mama pinned the hem of Sarah's new dress, I stared and wished I were Sarah.

When we left, I hung both dresses in the backseat of the car.

"It was sweet of Sarah to give you that dress," Mama said.

I looked at the two dresses hanging together. Somehow, the old one didn't seem so pretty anymore.

At home Mama had me try it on. It hung loosely like a sack. "It looks awful!" I complained.

Mama pinned and tucked, then took the dress to her room. "I'll fix it in time for graduation," she promised.

I didn't care. I could only think of Sarah's new dress. I dreamed
of having a dress like that. The more I dreamed, the more I wanted
something new.

A few Saturdays later, on the way to get groceries, Mama and I passed Tilly's Dress Shop. A white graduation dress hung in the window. It was as beautiful as Sarah's.

I begged Mama to let me try it on.

"We can't afford a new dress. There's no use…" Mama started.

I marched inside the store, not waiting for Mama to finish.

"How much is the dress in the window?" I asked the saleswoman.

She checked the price tag. "Eighty-five dollars," she said. "That's imported lace. Would you like to try it on?"

I felt sick. The eighty-five dollars might as well have been a thousand. "I…uh…" I stammered.

"No, thank you," said Mama calmly. She stood in the doorway. "It's too much for us."

"You could charge it," suggested the saleswoman.

Mama stiffened. "We pay cash as we go," she said. "Come on, Wynona. We need to get groceries."

It didn't seem right that Sarah could have a new dress but I couldn't. "It's not fair!" I yelled, storming from the store.

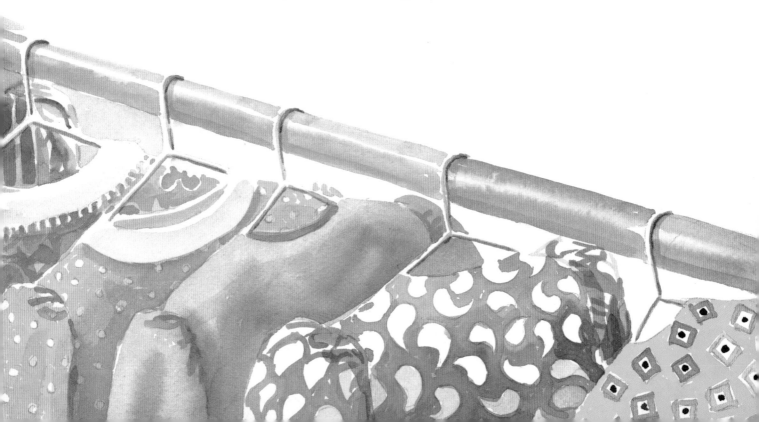

While we shopped for groceries, I begged Mama to let me apply
for a job so I could buy the dress myself. "You're too young for a job,
Wynona, and I need you to watch your brothers sometimes.
I already rely on our neighbors more than I should."

I didn't speak to Mama all the way home. I blamed her because
we couldn't afford the dress. I even blamed my two little brothers,
as if it were their fault I couldn't get a job.

The next day, when Mama came home from work, I raced to greet her. "I could earn money baby-sitting! And I could take Aaron and John Franklin with me!"

Mama sighed. "I'm afraid that won't do. Mrs. Culpepper says she needs me to work extra the next few weeks because she's having out-of-town company for graduation. I'll need you to help with the laundry and dinner."

My face turned red, and I shouted, "You just don't want me to get that dress!" Before Mama could speak, I ran from the room.

Every week on the way to buy groceries, we passed the dress
shop and I stared at the dress in the window, wishing I could have it.
Mama never said a word, but I knew she felt bad too.

Then, a week before graduation, as I carried Sarah's hemmed dress to the car, Mama handed me an envelope. "It's your graduation present."

I opened the envelope, and inside was enough money for the dress I'd been wanting!

"Tomorrow we'll go to town and buy that dress," Mama said. "If it needs altering, that will give me time to do it."

Tears welled up in my eyes. "You worked extra for me?"

"You'll be the prettiest girl at graduation," Mama said, pushing my hair from my face.

I noticed how tired she looked. Suddenly I felt ashamed. "I don't deserve—"

"Yes you do," Mama said, gathering me in her arms. I had a huge lump in my throat, and Mama held me for a moment.

"Now go wipe your face and watch your brothers. I'll deliver Sarah's dress."

I put the envelope in my pocket and went back inside. Sitting at the kitchen table, I daydreamed about wearing my beautiful new dress.

I was so busy thinking about myself, I forgot all about my brothers until I heard the scream. I raced to their bedroom. John Franklin was wailing and holding his wrist, which was twisted oddly.

Aaron's face was white. "We were just wrestling."

"It looks broken," I said. I carried John Franklin out front to wait for Mama. Aaron followed.

When Mama returned and saw us waiting, she must have realized something was wrong. She jumped from the car and ran over. "What…?" she started, stopping when she saw John Franklin's wrist.

"We'd better get to the hospital," she said. Her face looked tight, and I knew she was worried about more than just the broken wrist.

I reached into my pocket and handed her the envelope. "We can use this money for the hospital bill, Mama. I already have a dress."

She nodded, smiling sadly.

A few days later we signed John Franklin's cast, and Aaron and I helped him carry his books to school. The night before graduation, Mama stayed up late, and I knew she was finishing the alteration of Sarah's old dress. I didn't mind.

When I woke in the morning, the dress was hanging where I could see it. I went over for a closer look. It didn't even seem like the same dress! Mama had embroidered pale yellow roses all over it, scalloped the hem and waistline, and bought a yellow velvet ribbon for a sash. It was so pretty, I could hardly breathe.

I was running my fingers over the perfect tiny roses when Mama came in. "Oh, Mama, thank you, I love it! You made a whole new dress!" I threw my arms around her. "When did you find time to do all this?"

Mama kissed my forehead. "I'll always find time, Wynona."

And she does. That's Mama's way.